To the boy, the bug, and my lovie.
You are my heart.
—KK

To my wife, my sister, my parents,
and my *abuelas* for being a-maze-ing.
—LR

To my family.
—GB

WHEN *Pencil* MET

IMPRINT
A part of Macmillan Publishing Group, LLC
120 Broadway, New York, NY 10271

ABOUT THIS BOOK

The art for this book was created with pencil and paper (and eraser!), Photoshop, and Illustrator, using a Wacom Cintiq.
Text was set in Georgia and Avenir Next. For the title page, Timeout was used. It was edited by John Morgan and designed by Germán Blanco.
The production was supervised by Raymond Ernesto Colón, and the production editor was Dawn Ryan.

Printed in China by Toppan Leefung Printing Ltd., Dongguan City, Guangdong Province.

Library of Congress Control Number: 2018955951.

ISBN 978-1-250-30939-6 (hardcover)

Our books may be purchased in bulk for promotional, educational, or business use. Please contact your local bookseller or the Macmillan Corporate and Premium Sales Department at (800) 221-7945 ext. 5442 or by email at MacmillanSpecialMarkets@macmillan.com.

Imprint logo designed by Amanda Spielman

First edition, 2019

5 7 9 10 8 6

mackids.com

WHEN *Pencil* MET ERASER

Story by Karen Kilpatrick and Luis O. Ramos, Jr.
Illustrated by Germán Blanco

New York

Once, there was a pencil . . .

who loved to draw.

Pencil liked to work alone.

Whatchya
doin'?

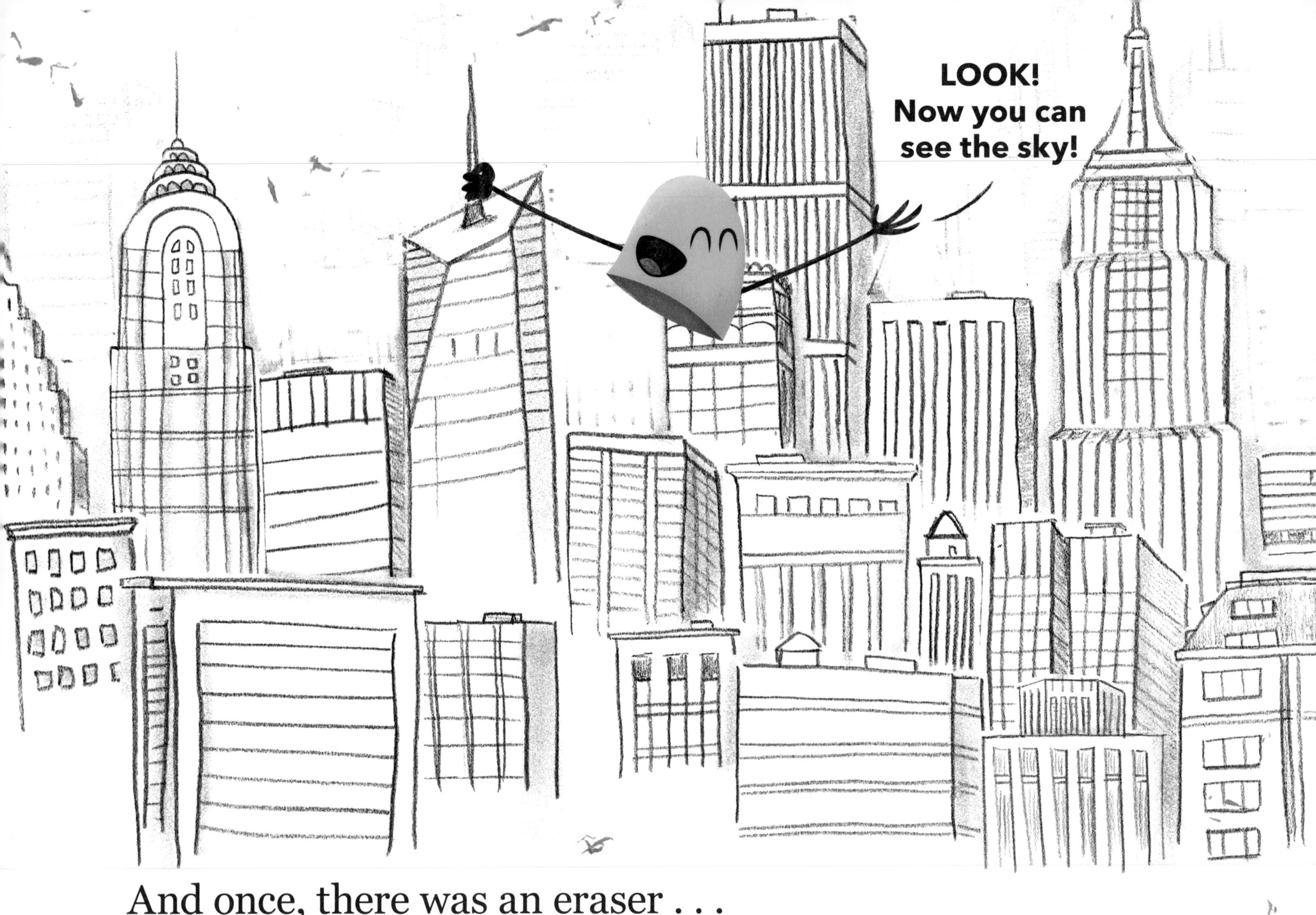

And once, there was an eraser . . .

who loved to erase!

But Pencil wasn't very
happy about it.

Let's do
another one!

Leave the ART
to the artist.

Pencil kept drawing.

And Eraser kept erasing.

Look! Now we can walk through the meadow!

And drawing.

And erasing.
Look! Now it's
smooth sailing.

Pencil didn’t think his ART needed erasing to be great.

But Eraser had other ideas.

Bet you can't make
EVERYTHING better. See what
you can do with this!

And this?

Everyone knows that a pencil
can never resist a maze . . .

but sometimes pencils
make mistakes . . .

and erasers can help fix them!

You know, maybe we ARE better together! COME ON!!!

And you know what?

They were.

I'm sticking
with YOU from
now on!

Once, there was a pencil
AND an eraser . . .

who loved to create.

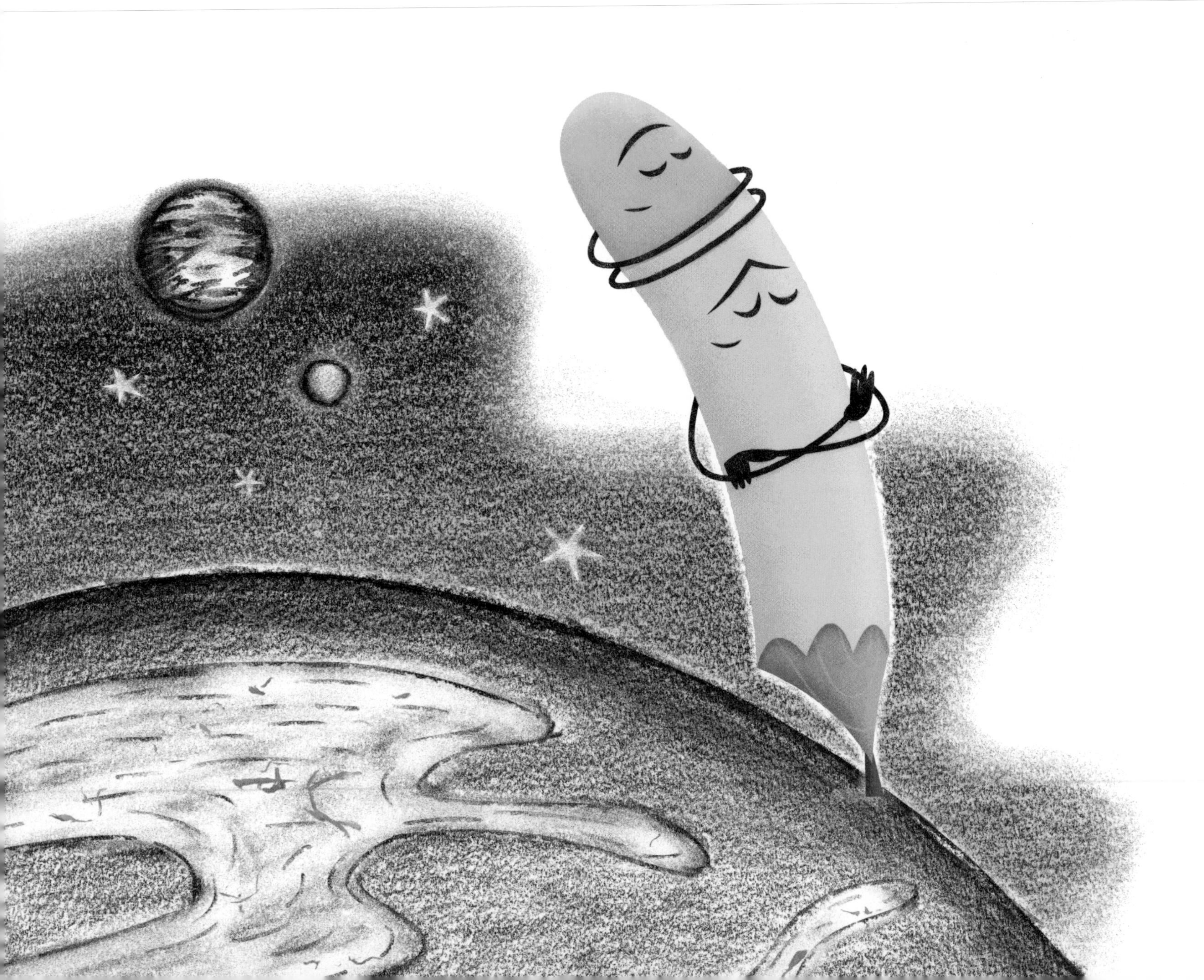

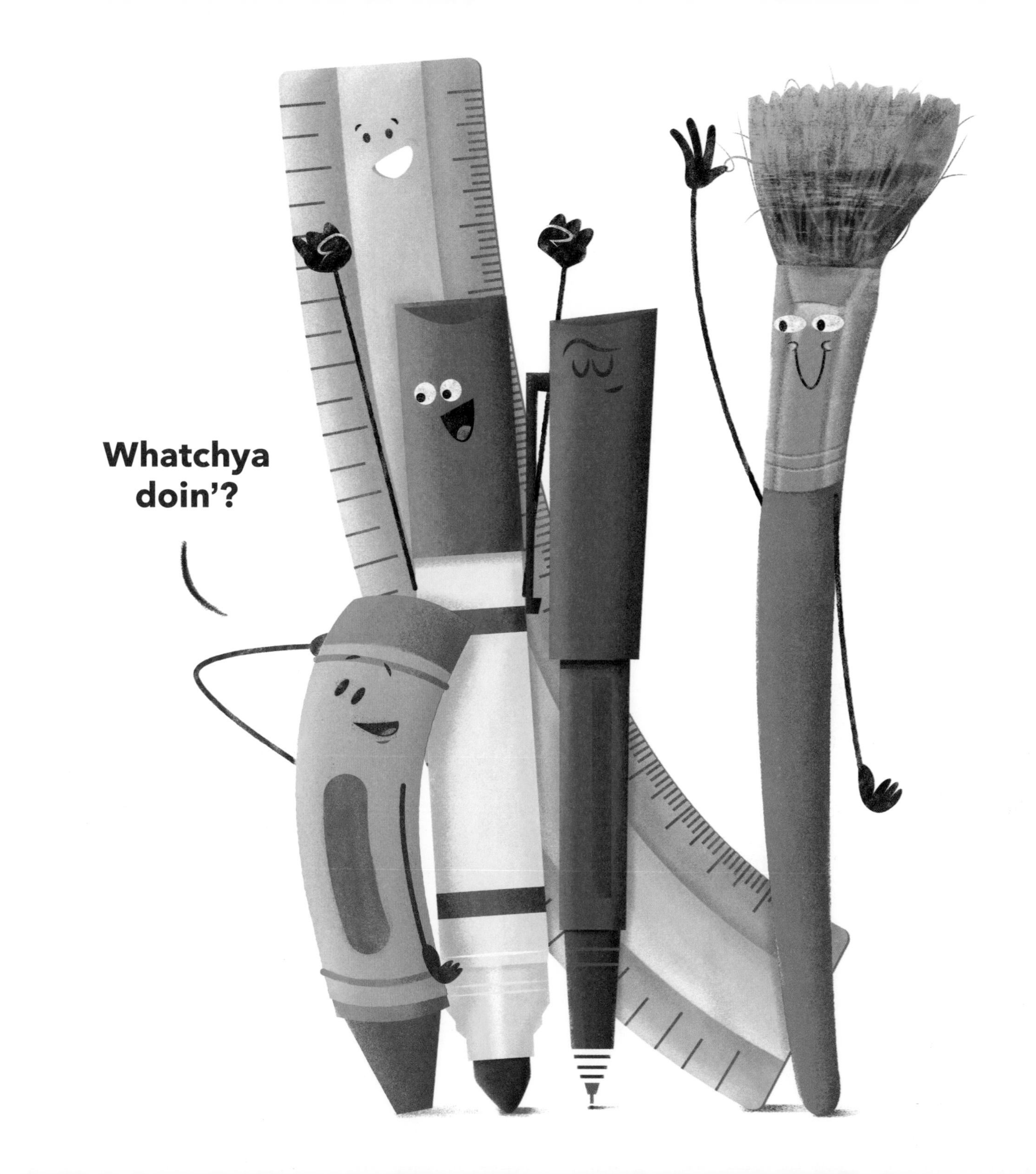
Whatchya
doin'?

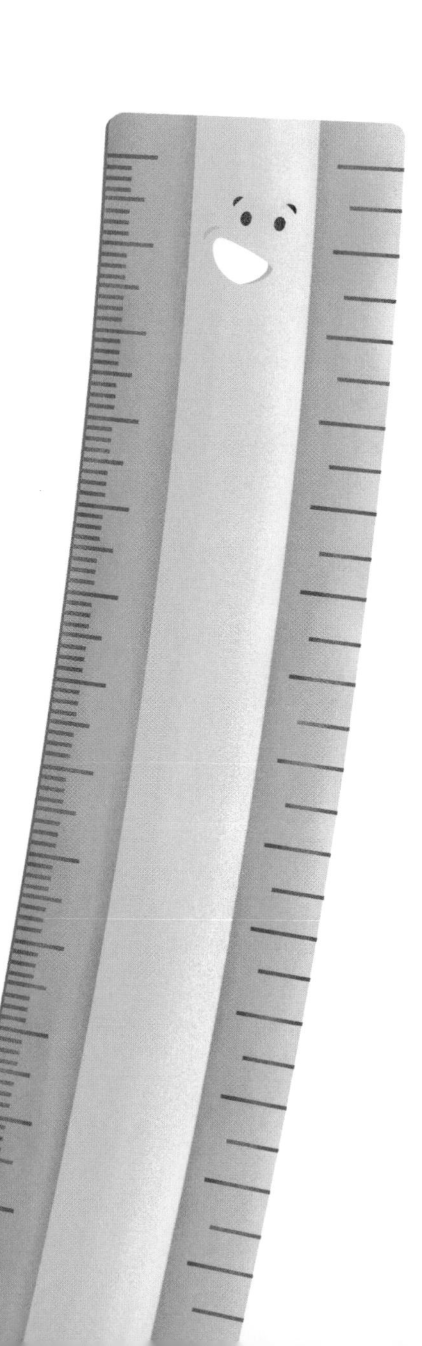

The End?

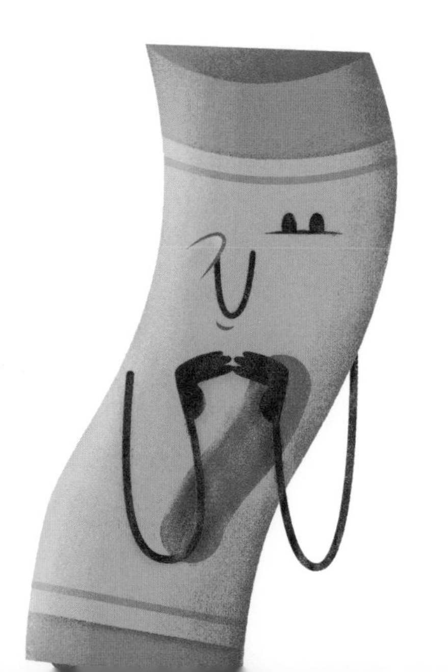

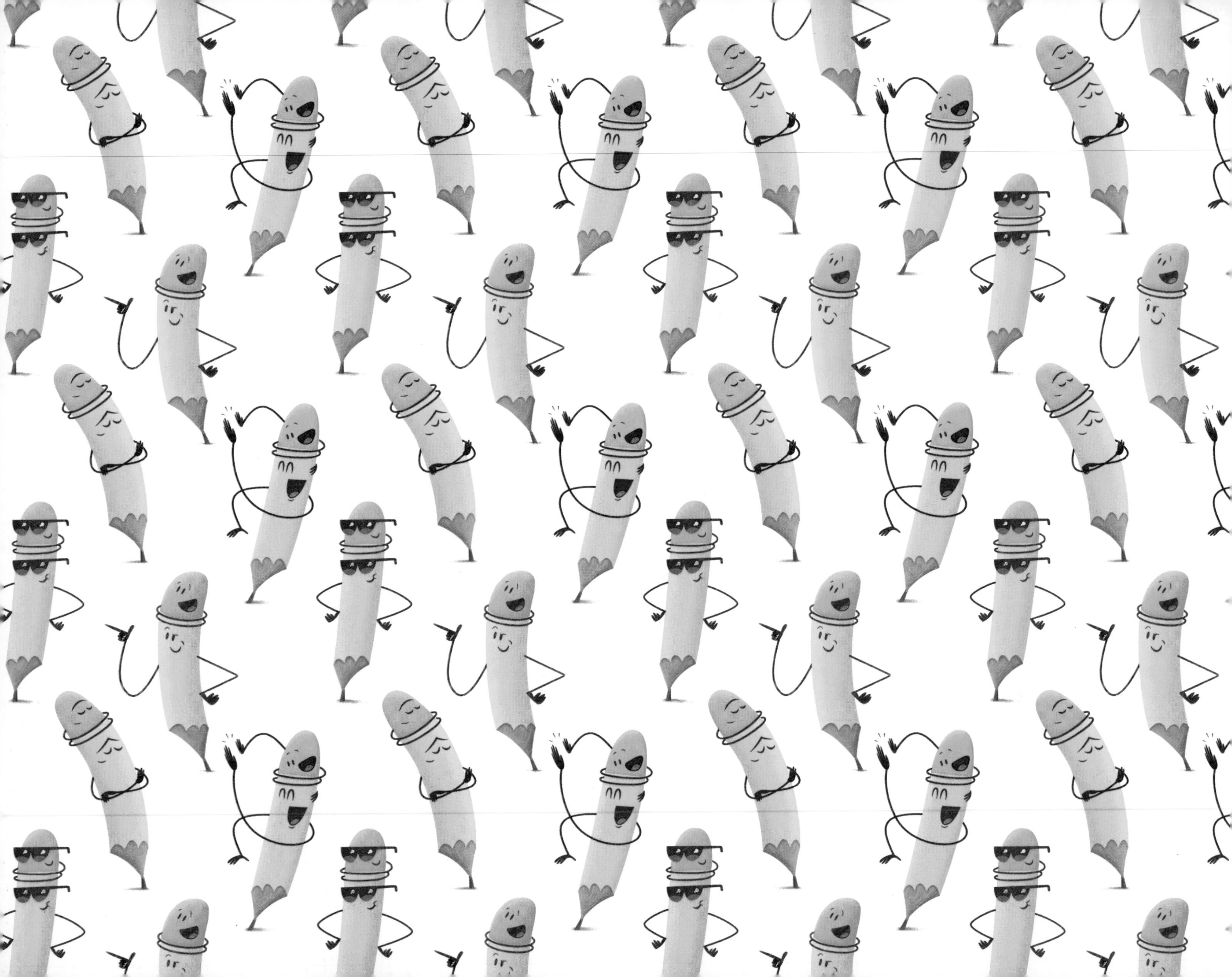